This igloo book belongs to:

....

igloobooks

Published in 2016
by Igloo Books Ltd
Cottage Farm
Sywell
NN6 0BJ
www.igloobooks.com

GUA006 0216
2 4 6 8 10 9 7 5 3 1
ISBN: 978-1-78557-428-3

Printed and manufactured in China

My Treasury of Classic Fairy Tales

igloobooks

Contents

The Little Mermaid

Long ago, in the watery depths of the bluest ocean, a little mermaid lived with her five sisters and their father, the sea king. All day long, the little mermaid played among the bright blooms of the sea gardens and listened to her sisters telling stories about the world beyond the sea. "I love my home," said the little mermaid, "but I wish I could see the world above the waves."

Then, on her fifteenth birthday, the sea king said that the little mermaid could go to the water's surface and see everything her sisters had seen. The little mermaid was very excited. She waved goodbye to her family and rose, as lightly as a bubble, to the surface.

Above the water, the sun was setting. Clouds glowed red and gold in the glimmering twilight. As the little mermaid looked around in wonder, she saw a large ship on which finely dressed people were laughing and dancing. Swimming closer, she learned that they were celebrating the birthday of a handsome young prince. The little mermaid was enchanted when she saw the prince and could not take her eyes off him.

As the hours passed by, the sea became restless. The ship's sails began to billow and the waves began to rise higher and higher. Heavy clouds darkened the sky and jagged lightning flashed.

Soon, a terrible storm struck, and the ship creaked and groaned. Huge, crashing waves tore at the mast and ripped it in two. The little mermaid watched as the prince was flung into the sea and sank beneath the waves. "I must rescue him," she thought. "Otherwise he will surely die."

The little mermaid dove down and pulled the prince up to the surface. She held him tightly until the storm ceased and she kissed his forehead tenderly. Then, she swam with him to a distant beach. The little mermaid left the prince safely on the shore and swam off to hide behind nearby rocks until he awoke.

After many hours of waiting, the little mermaid saw a pretty, young girl come down to the beach. She ran to the half-drowned prince and held him until he opened his eyes. The prince smiled up at the girl, as if she had been the one who had rescued him. Watching from afar, the little mermaid's heart sank, for her handsome prince did not know that it was she who had saved him from the stormy sea. She dove sorrowfully down into the ocean and returned to her underwater home.

As she sat in her lonely sea garden, the little mermaid thought how she would happily trade her life at the bottom of the ocean for just one day with her prince on land.

The Little Mermaid

Soon, her longing to see the prince became too much for the little mermaid. "I will visit the sea witch," she said. "Even though I am afraid of her, she has powerful magic that can surely help me." So, the little mermaid flicked her tail and set off, down into the coldest, darkest waters that led to the seaweed forest and the home of the sea witch.

In a house made of bones, the little mermaid found the sea witch. She told the witch her story of the prince and how she wished to find him. "Can you help me?" asked the little mermaid.

The Little Mermaid

The sea witch cackled. "Drink this potion and you will become human and find your way to your prince," she said. "However, in return, you must give me your voice."

The little mermaid agreed and drank the potion. She swam up through the blue water and as she reached the surface, the mermaid felt her tail change into two legs. She was able to walk on land, but she could not utter a single sound. The little mermaid would never be able to tell the prince how much she loved him. In despair, she fell at the foot of the marble steps that led to the prince's palace.

The Little Mermaid

It wasn't long before the handsome prince found the little mermaid. He thought she was a poor beggar and took pity on her. The prince gave her fine clothes and treated her as if she were his sister. Each day, he took her riding through the sweet-scented woods and each day, she fell more and more deeply in love with the prince, but the little mermaid could not speak a word of it to him. "You are very dear to me," said the prince one day, "but my father wishes me to marry. I must sail at dawn tomorrow to meet a princess of my father's choosing."

The Little Mermaid

The little mermaid traveled with the prince to the kingdom where the princess lived. In the streets, bells rang and trumpets blew. The princess appeared and the prince recognized her instantly. "You are the girl from the beach who rescued me," he said. "I have loved you since the first moment I saw you, but I never thought we would meet again. Now we are to be married!" With that, the happy prince took the princess in his arms and kissed her.

The little mermaid was heartbroken. When no one was looking, she dove back into the sea. As the water covered her legs, they transformed back into a silvery fishtail again. Her voice was restored and she swam down, down into the watery depths singing her sad song.

The Little Mermaid

The little mermaid sobbed in the arms of her father, the sea king. He hugged her tightly and said, "There, there, child. Do not waste your tears on what is not meant to be. You may have been happy for a while on land, but your heart would have cried out for the ocean. You are a mermaid and your home is under the sea. You belong here with us."

The little mermaid's sisters wiped away her tears and combed her hair. Then, they swam with her to the surface and watched as the handsome prince and his beautiful princess were married. "Goodbye," said the little mermaid, sadly, and she gave a flick of her golden tail and dove under the gently lapping waves.

The little mermaid was soon happy again in her underwater home. All day long, she sang and played in the sea gardens and made shell necklaces. On days when the sea was rough and stormy, she thought of her handsome prince.

As for the prince, he often wondered what had happened to the lovely girl who had been like a sister to him. He recalled how, on the day of his wedding, he had thought that he saw an image of the girl's face, just for a moment, in the rippling waters. He remembered seeing a slight glint of shimmering gold that seemed to grow smaller and smaller as it disappeared down, down into the mysterious depths of the deep, blue ocean.

The Princess and the Pea

Once upon a time, there was a handsome prince who wanted, more than anything in the world, to find a beautiful princess to marry. The prince traveled far and wide and met lots of princesses from many different lands, but none of them ever seemed to be quite what he was looking for.

Feeling very downhearted and weary from traveling, the disappointed prince returned home to the royal palace. He sat by the window of his lonely tower, wishing that there was a way that he could find the perfect princess to marry.

Then, one dark night, a terrible storm raged across the kingdom. Lightning bolts flashed across the sky and thunder boomed, as the wind howled and moaned. Rain clattered and battered against the windowpanes and ran in rivulets down the drenched rooftops.

Suddenly, there came the sound of knocking at the palace door. "Who could possibly be out on such a night?" said the king as he hurried to find out who it was. As the palace door opened with a creak, the king saw a discheveled girl standing on the doorstep.

"Good heavens," said the king, looking very startled, for the wind and the rain had made the girl look as though she had just climbed out of the river. The water ran down from her hair and clothes. It trickled into the toes of her shoes and spilled over the heels into little puddles. "I beg your pardon for calling so late," said the girl, "but I have come to ask you to help me. I am a princess and I am lost in this storm. Please, will you give me shelter for the night?"

"Of course," said the king. "Come in, my dear."

Nearby, the queen was listening. It would be very nice if her son could at last find a wife, but the queen needed to know if this mysterious girl truly was a princess. So, she tiptoed upstairs to one of the royal bedchambers. "Put a single pea on the base of this bed," the queen commanded her servants, "then lay twenty mattresses on top of it."

One by one, the mattresses were stacked upon the pea. What a job the servants had! At last, the task was complete and it was time for everyone to go to bed.

~ ☙ *The Princess and the Pea* ❧ ~

The princess lay all night on the tall pile of mattresses. In the morning, the king and queen came to the girl's bedchamber to ask how she had slept.

"Oh, I slept very badly!" replied the girl. "I tossed and turned all night and hardly closed my eyes. The bed looked so very comfortable, but it felt like I was lying on something hard. I may as well have been sleeping on a stone!"

The queen was very happy. Only a true princess could be so sensitive as to feel a single pea beneath twenty mattresses. It seemed that her son might have found a wife after all.

The prince came down from his tower and fell instantly in love with the beautiful girl.
He was very happy because at last he had found a true princess. The prince would soon marry the
princess and they would live happily, ever after.

The king and the queen were very happy, too. After many years of searching, their only son had
found a wife. They no longer needed the pea, but because it had been so useful, they decided to put
it into a museum and as far as anyone knows, it is still there to this very day.

Little Red Riding Hood

Long ago, there was a young girl whose grandmother gave her a little, red cape with a hood. The girl loved the red cape so much and wore it so often, everyone called her Little Red Riding Hood.

One day, Little Red Riding Hood's mother said, "Your grandmother is ill and it would make her feel much better if you were to take this basket of lovely cakes to her."
"Of course," said Little Red Riding Hood. She was very happy to take the delicious cakes to her grandmother, who lived in the middle of a deep, dark woods.

So, Little Red Riding Hood took the basket of cakes and said goodbye to her mother. She set off from their little cottage and made her way towards the woods. "Stay on the path," called out her mother, waving, "and remember, don't talk to strangers."

In the woods, shafts of sunlight shone from above. Old trees creaked and groaned and made strange shadows on the path. "What a lovely day," said Little Red Riding Hood as she admired the pretty flowers along the path. She hadn't gone far, when a dark shape stepped out from behind a gnarled old tree. "Good afternoon," said a big gray wolf, smiling. "Where might you be off to on such a beautiful day, little girl?"

"I am taking this basket of cakes to my granny who is ill," replied Little Red Riding Hood.
The wolf grinned wickedly and his dark eyes glinted. He was very hungry and he wanted more than just a snack. The sly wolf licked his lips and thought to himself that Granny would make a tasty supper and this tender girl, a mouth-watering dessert. If he was very clever, he could eat them both.

So, the wolf walked with Little Red Riding Hood until they came to a pretty patch of flowers, lit by a beam of sunlight. "Why don't you pick some flowers for your granny?" suggested the wolf.

Little Red Riding Hood

Little Red Riding Hood forgot all about what her mother had said and stepped off the path to pick some flowers. Without a word, the crafty wolf slipped away unseen and bounded through the woods to Granny's house. *Tap-tap*, he went on her cottage door and spoke in a high, girlish voice. "It's Little Red Riding Hood, Granny, please may I come in?" he said.
"Of course you can come in, my dear," replied Granny.

The wolf flung open the door and with a growl, he leapt towards the bed. He meant to gobble Granny up and he was just about to take a big, juicy bite out of her when he heard Little Red Riding Hood coming. The clever wolf pushed Granny into a cupboard, then he quickly put on one of her nightgowns and a nightcap and jumped into bed.

Little Red Riding Hood

Rat-a-tat-tat, went Little Red Riding Hood on the door of Granny's cottage.

"Come in my dear," said the wolf in his best Granny voice.

The little door creaked open and Little Red Riding Hood peered at the figure in the bed.

She stopped for a moment and looked at her grandmother. Little Red Riding Hood frowned.

"Granny, what big eyes you have," she said.

"All the better to see you with, my dear," said the wolf.

"Gosh, what big ears you have, Granny," said Little Red Riding Hood.

"All the better to hear you with," said the wolf, pulling the sheets down a little.

Little Red Riding Hood moved closer to the bed. "Granny, what big, white, sharp, pointy teeth you have," she said.

"All the better to EAT you with!" growled the wolf. Suddenly, he threw back the sheets and leapt out of the bed at Little Red Riding Hood. "Grrrr!"

The hungry wolf chased Little Red Riding Hood all over Granny's cottage. There was a terrible commotion. What a noise they made! *Crash* went the upturned table. *Smash* went Granny's best china onto the stone floor. Around and around went Little Red Riding Hood and the hungry wolf. "Help!" cried the little girl, afraid she was about to be eaten.

Outside, a woodcutter, who happened to be passing, heard the awful noise. "I bet that wolf is up to no good again," he said, for the woodcutter knew all about the cunning wolf and his sly ways. "I'll soon put a stop to that," said the woodcutter. He grabbed his ax and burst into Granny's cottage.

Little Red Riding Hood

The wolf was just about to gobble up Little Red Riding Hood whole. His huge mouth opened and his white teeth glistened. "Stop right there," said the woodcutter. "I fancy a juicy bit of wolf for my supper tonight." His ax blade glinted and in it the wolf saw his own reflection. He stared up at the woodcutter who glared back fiercely. "Be on your way, wolf," he said.

The woodcutter leaned a little bit closer to the wolf, so that the sharp ax blade almost touched his nose. The wolf gulped and gave a cowardly whimper. Then, with one big leap, he bounded out of the cottage and into the dark woods.

Little Red Riding Hood let Granny out of the cupboard. "There, there, Granny," she said, giving her a big hug. "That nasty wolf is gone now."

Little Red Riding Hood

Granny and Little Red Riding Hood thanked the woodcutter. If it hadn't been for him, then who knows what would have happened? "Let's have a nice, hot drink," said Granny, "and some of these lovely cakes that Little Red Riding Hood brought all this way for me."

So, the woodcutter, Granny, and Little Red Riding Hood sat together outside, in the warm sunshine and ate the delicious cakes. "Thank you for making me feel better," said Granny to Little Red Riding Hood, "and protecting me from that awful wolf."

After that, whenever Little Red Riding Hood went to see her grandmother, she always stayed on the path and she never, ever, talked to strangers again. As for the wolf, he is still out there somewhere, skulking in the shadows. It is wise to remember that, should you ever go walking in the dark woods alone.

Cinderella

Long ago, there lived a beautiful girl who had a wicked stepmother and two spiteful stepsisters. They were jealous of the girl because not only was she beautiful, she was also patient and kind. "From now on, you will sleep in the kitchen and do the housework," said the cruel stepmother. She took all of the girl's pretty clothes away and made her wear a ragged, old dress. From then on, the girl cooked and cleaned and lit the fires. The stepmother and her daughters laughed at her because she was always dirty from sweeping cinders from the grate. "We will call you Cinderella," they said.

As it happened, the king commanded that there should be a great ball in the royal palace. To each and every household in the kingdom, he sent a special invitation. The stepmother and her daughters were dizzy with excitement. "You must help us to prepare," they said to Cinderella. "You must comb our hair and fasten our buttons, for we shall wear the finest satins and silks." "You could go, too, Cinderella," said the wicked stepmother, "but you have nothing nice to wear and in any case, you are so very dirty." At this, the stepsisters waved the invitation in the air and laughed cruelly at poor Cinderella.

As the stepmother and stepsisters left for the ball, tears trickled down Cinderella's cheeks.

"Oh, if only I wasn't so dirty and ragged," she sobbed. "If only I too could dance in a fine dress at the splendid royal ball."

Suddenly, there was a bright flash of light and a shining figure appeared. "Good evening, my dear," said a soft voice. "I am your fairy godmother and you shall go to the ball, Cinderella. Fetch me a pumpkin, four white mice, and two small, black rats."

"How can these things take me to the ball?" asked Cinderella.

The fairy godmother waved her wand. "Like this," she said, smiling. *Poof!* Suddenly, the pumpkin became a sparkling, golden coach. *Poof!* The mice became four magnificent white horses and the rats, two elegant footmen.

Cinderella was delighted and amazed, but then she remembered her grubby dress. "I can't go to the ball like this," she said, sadly.

The fairy godmother smiled and waved her wand again. *Poof!* Cinderella's ragged dress transformed into a shimmering ball gown that glittered and shone with jewels. On her feet were the most delicate glass slippers that glinted and gleamed in the moonlight. "Go to the ball, Cinderella," said the fairy godmother, "but leave before the clock strikes twelve, otherwise all the magic will disappear."

❦ Cinderella ❦

The magical coach carried Cinderella all the way to the royal palace. Inside, enchanting music played as finely-dressed people whirled and twirled at the sumptuous ball. When Cinderella entered the ballroom, everyone gasped in astonishment. They all wondered who this beautiful girl was and where she had come from.

The prince was captivated by his mystery guest and as soon as she arrived, he asked her to dance. All night long, the prince and Cinderella danced together. Cinderella was happier than she could ever remember because it seemed that all her dreams had come true. Then, the clock struck twelve.

Suddenly, Cinderella remembered what the fairy godmother had said. If she stayed any longer, her beautiful dress would turn back to rags. "I must go," she said to the prince and with that, Cinderella dashed out of the ballroom and down the palace steps. "Wait!" cried the prince, running after her, but Cinderella had gone.

All that was left was a single, delicate glass slipper, lying on the cold, stone steps.
"I will not rest until I find the girl whose foot fits this slipper," said the prince, "and when I do, she shall be my wife."

The prince searched all over the kingdom, but found no one whom the slipper fitted. Finally, he came to the house where Cinderella lived. The spoiled stepsisters pushed forward, convinced that they would be successful. "Ouch, ouch!" they cried as each one tried to squeeze a big foot into the delicate slipper, only to find it did not fit. "Who else lives here?" asked the prince.

"Just Cinderella," replied the stepmother, "but the slipper couldn't possibly fit her!"

"*Everyone* shall try the slipper," commanded the prince. "Go and fetch Cinderella."

Sure enough, when Cinderella tried on the slipper, it fit like a glove.

∽ • Cinderella • ∽

The prince asked Cinderella to marry him and she accepted. She would have forgiven her stepmother and stepsisters for all the awful things they had done, but they were so jealous of her good fortune, they left the kingdom and never returned.

So, Cinderella married the prince. The birds sang and the sun shone. Cinderella was happier than she had ever been. Never again would she sweep the cinders from the grate or wear dirty, ragged clothes. Now she was a real princess and she would live happily ever after with her very own handsome prince.

The Emperor's New Clothes

Long ago, there lived an emperor who loved nothing more than dressing up in fine, expensive clothes. As soon as he had bought one thing, however, he just wanted another. The emperor never gave a thought to his poor subjects. All he cared about was spending money on new clothes. Then, one day, two swindlers arrived in the kingdom. They told people that they were weavers who could make the most incredible cloth. The swindlers said that this cloth was not only beautiful, but it was invisible to any person who was unfit to do his job or who wasn't very clever.

Before long, the emperor came to hear about the amazing cloth. "I want to see these weavers, immediately," he commanded. "With this cloth, I can have more new clothes and find out which of my subjects are stupid and unable to do their jobs!"

Within an hour, the swindlers arrived at the grand palace. They were given money, silk, and the most expensive golden thread for the cloth. The cunning pair used none of the things they had been given, but instead kept them for themselves. They sat at two empty looms and pretended to work until long into the night.

The emperor became impatient to see the incredible new cloth. Then, suddenly, he began to worry. "What if I can't see it?" he thought. "My subjects will hear of it and think I'm not fit to be king." So, the clever king sent his most trusted minister to see if the cloth was ready.

The minister went into the room where the swindlers sat at their looms. "Here is the cloth for the emperor's new suit," they said. The minister peered at the looms and frowned, for he could not see anything. "Can you not see the beautiful fabric and its intricate design?" asked the swindlers.

The minister did not see anything because there was nothing there to see. However, he was so worried about telling anyone, that he pretended he could see the cloth, exactly as the swindlers had described. "Oh, it is the finest, most beautiful cloth I have ever seen!" he cried.

After that, the emperor decided to see the cloth for himself. The swindlers convinced him of its beauty and refinement. The emperor, fearing he might be thought unfit to rule, or even worse, very stupid, said, "Oh, yes, it is the finest cloth I have ever seen. It is so fine, I want you to make me a suit, so that I can parade it through the kingdom."

The Emperor's New Clothes

The two swindlers pretended to cut the invisible cloth. Then, they pretended to sew it with needles that had no thread. Soon, they announced that the suit was ready. "Here are the trousers," they said. "Here is the coat and a cloak, too."

The swindlers handed the invisible suit around to the emperor's courtiers. "Feel how light it is," they said. "It is the most incredible cloth you will ever see."
"It is lighter than air," the courtiers all agreed, for they too were afraid to say that they could see nothing at all.
"We would ask you to undress, your Majesty," said the swindlers, "so that we might fit your new suit and show everyone how marvelous you look in it."

The Emperor's New Clothes

All the courtiers looked on as the emperor took off his clothes and stood in his underwear. Meanwhile, the swindlers pretended to put on the pieces of the new suit. "How well they look!" cried the courtiers. "How wonderfully they fit, Majesty!"

The emperor looked at his reflection in the mirror. He saw nothing but his underwear, but because he was too afraid to say anything, for fear of being judged, he simply smiled and said, "I am ready for my parade." With that, he led the way outside into the narrow streets of the town.

The Emperor's New Clothes

The people of the kingdom had heard all about the emperor's incredible, new suit. They had heard that if they could not see it, then it meant they were not good subjects or even worse, that they were very stupid. So, there was much cheering and clapping as they saw the emperor approaching. "What a marvelous suit!" they cried. "How well it fits him!" Not a single person wished the other to know that, in fact, they could see nothing at all.

Suddenly, a little boy stood out from the crowd. He pointed up at the emperor and said, "Look, Mother. He's only wearing his underpants!"

The Emperor's New Clothes

The crowd went quiet and the little boy spoke again. "Mother," he said. "The emperor's parading through the town in his underwear!" The little boy began to laugh. The emperor looked down at himself. At first, he looked puzzled. Then, he looked annoyed. After a while, however, he too began to laugh. Before long, everyone was laughing. The emperor realized that he had been tricked by the swindlers, but he wasn't cross. "What a proud and foolish man I have been," he said. "Forgive me, my loyal subjects." After that, the emperor put his real clothes on and commanded that everyone should have a great big party.

The Ugly Duckling

It was summer in the country and golden corn ripened in the fields. Near a sleepy little farm, on the banks of a river, a mother duck settled down on her nest of eggs. She sat patiently until suddenly, one of the egg shells began to crack. Soon, another one cracked, and then another. One by one, tiny heads poked out. *Peep, peep, quack, quack,* went the little ducklings as they looked around.

Soon, all the eggs had hatched, except for one. This egg was much larger than the others. "Maybe it's a turkey egg," said an old duck who had come to have a look.

The mother duck didn't like the idea of a turkey egg in her nest, but nevertheless she settled back down to keep it warm.

Sometime later, there was a soft, cracking sound. It got louder and louder until suddenly, a fluffy head poked out of the egg, then a body. This duckling was not at all like the others. It was very large, gray, and ugly. "Maybe it is a turkey after all," said the mother duck. "I shall take it to the river and see if it can swim like my other babies."

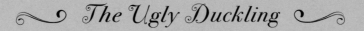

The mother duck took her ducklings down to the river. One after another, they plopped into the water with a *splash!* The ugly duckling jumped in, too. "He swims just like the others," said the mother duck, "I am sure he must be mine. He's just a bit different, that's all."

The ducklings had a lovely time swimming in the cool water. Soon, the mother duck decided that it was time for them to meet the animals in the farmyard. "I shall see what they think of my new family," she thought and she waddled up the bank, with all the ducklings following behind her.

The Ugly Duckling

In the farmyard, the hens and geese looked at the new arrivals. "What's that one at the end?" they cried, laughing. "He looks so ugly!" The other farm animals all gathered around. They too thought the duckling was very ugly. They didn't like him at all.

The poor little duckling was pushed, bitten, and made fun of. After a while, his mother began to ignore him and even his brothers and sisters began to bully him. "You're so ugly," they cried. The ugly duckling was chased this way and that. The other ducks pecked him so much that he ran away from the farm as fast as his legs could carry him.

"They are afraid of me because I am ugly," said the sad little duckling and he hid in the thick reeds of the marshes where no one would see him. Soon, hunters with fierce dogs came. The dogs ran past the little duckling, but they did not hurt him. "Even those fierce dogs think I am too ugly to bite," said the sad ugly duckling and he left the marsh to walk over the fields. The little duckling walked a very long way. He was hungry and tired, when he came to a little cottage by a woods where an old woman lived.

The Ugly Duckling

The old woman thought she might get some eggs from the duckling, so she let him stay. In her cottage, there was a cat who could purr and a hen who could cluck. They didn't mind the ugly duckling staying, as long as he behaved just like them.

Time passed and soon the duckling felt the urge to swim. "You don't want to do that," said the cat and the hen. "You should forget all about swimming and be like us." The ugly duckling couldn't purr like the cat, or cluck like the hen. "I do not belong here," he thought, sadly and he left the little cottage.

The Ugly Duckling

In the rippling waters of a river, the ugly duckling swam and dived. The other animals avoided him because of his ugliness and he was very lonely. One day, a flock of beautiful, white birds flew across the sky. Their dazzling beauty made the ugly duckling's heart leap and a longing stirred in him that he could not explain, but he had no one to tell.

Soon, the bitter cold of winter fell upon the land. The reeds and river froze and the little duckling was trapped by ice and snow. Luckily for him, a kind man was passing by. He pulled the shivering duckling from the ice and took him home.

The Ugly Duckling

"Look what I found in the river," said the man to his children. He set the duckling down by the fire and the heat revived him. The man's children were very excited. They wanted to play with the duckling, but the poor creature was very afraid. He flapped his wings as the children chased him around. First the duckling knocked over the milk bucket, then he bumped into a sack of corn. "Stop! Stop!" screeched the man's wife. The poor duckling was so frightened, he ran out through the open door into the falling snow.

The Ugly Duckling

It is sad to think how the little duckling suffered through that long, dark winter. There was not a friend to listen to his troubles. Just as he thought he couldn't bear his loneliness any longer, the first rays of spring sunshine shone down. The duckling's wings were strengthened by the soothing warmth and, as he flapped them, they carried him up into the air. Just as he was flying above a large garden, the duckling noticed three beautiful birds floating on a lake below. "I will fly to those birds," he said to himself. "They might tease and bully me because I am so ugly, but it would be better to try and befriend them than to be pecked by ducks, frightened by hunters and children, or frozen by the cruel winter."

The Ugly Duckling

So, the ugly duckling flew down to the white birds. He bowed his head before them and waited for their first cruel words, just as he had come to expect from the other creatures. Then, in the rippling water, he saw his own reflection. It wasn't that of a gray, ugly duckling, but a graceful, gleaming swan. All the other swans gathered around to welcome him. Children ran to the water's edge and gasped at the sight of the handsome new arrival. The humble swan lowered his head shyly. At last, he had found where he belonged. Never again would he be seen as the ugly duckling, for now he was truly a beautiful swan.

Hansel and Gretel

Long ago, a woodcutter lived with his two children, Hansel and Gretel and his new wife. They were so poor, there was hardly enough food to eat. "What will become of us?" said the woodcutter.

"Unless we are all to starve, you must take the children to the thickest part of the woods and leave them there," said the cruel wife, for she was the children's stepmother and did not care for them as their real mother had.

The woodcutter felt sorry for his children, but he feared his wife and agreed to do as she said. Hansel and Gretel overheard their stepmother's plans and Gretel began to cry.
"We will surely die," she sobbed, but her brother comforted her.
"I have a plan, Sister, so sleep soundly, for all is not lost," he said.

The next morning, Hansel put a piece of bread into his pocket. As the woodcutter led the children into the woods, Hansel crumbled the bread and sprinkled a trail along the floor behind him.

Deep in the forest, the woodcutter built a fire. "Rest here, children," he said and as soon as Hansel and Gretel had fallen asleep, their father left them in the woods, alone.

When they woke, night had fallen and the moon shone brightly. "Do not worry," said Hansel, "for we shall follow the trail of crumbs I left earlier." When they looked, however, they saw that the forest birds had eaten every crumb and there was no trail left to follow.

Hansel and Gretel

The children wandered deeper into the woods. "We are lost," said Gretel. "We will never find our way home." Just then, Hansel saw a white dove sitting in the trees. It cooed softly and took flight.

The bird was so beautiful that the little children followed it until it landed on the roof of a curious-looking house. The walls were made of thick gingerbread covered with frosting and the window panes were clear sugar. The roof was made of candy, so Hansel reached up and pulled some off. "Mmm, delicious," he said. Gretel licked the frosting off of a piece of gingerbread and the two children giggled and soon began to forget about their troubles.

Suddenly, the door of the cottage flew open and an old woman appeared in the doorway. "Come in," she said, "for I have more sweets and lots of lovely treats inside."

The children were very hungry, so they stepped inside. The old woman, however, had fooled them, for she was really a witch who liked nothing more than to devour plump, little children. As soon as Hansel and Gretel entered the cottage, the witch slammed the door with a *thud!* "Now you are my prisoners!" cackled the witch. "You will make tasty morsels for me when I am hungry and feel like a nice, juicy snack."

The witch grabbed Hansel and locked him in a cage. "When you are good and fat, I shall cook you for my supper," she shrieked. Then, she ordered Gretel to sweep the house and make the best food to fatten up her brother.

Each day, the witch went to Hansel's cage. "Hold out your finger and I shall see how fat you have grown," she said. Each day, clever Hansel held out a little chicken bone and because the witch's eyesight was poor, she did not notice that it was not his finger at all.

After some weeks, the witch grew impatient that Hansel was not growing any fatter. "Whether he be fat or lean, I shall eat him anyway," she said.

Hansel and Gretel

"Before I cook your brother, I need to make sure that there is plenty of room in the oven," the witch said to Gretel. "Creep in, my dear." Gretel was clever, just like her brother and knew that the witch planned to cook her in the oven. "Oh, but I need your help," she said. "I do not know how to climb in. Please will you show me?"

"What a silly goose you are!" cried the witch to Gretel. "It is easy to get in. Look, I shall show you." With that, the witch began to climb into the oven. No sooner had she done so, than Gretel shoved her in and slammed the door shut.

"I shall not cook you, Witch, as you would have done to me," said Gretel, "but here in the oven you shall stay until we are far away."

Gretel freed Hansel from his cage and the two children hugged one another. "We must run from this place," said Hansel, "but first we shall fill our pockets with jewels and gold, for the witch has chests full of treasure."

So, the children took as much treasure as they could carry and fled from the cottage, leaving the witch cursing behind them. "How will we find our way home?" Gretel asked her brother.

Suddenly, the white dove the children had seen earlier flew overhead. It cooed softly and Hansel and Gretel followed the bird along the winding pathways of the great woods, until at last they saw their father's cottage.

The woodcutter was so happy to see his children that he wept tears of joy. He hugged them tightly and begged them to forgive him for leaving them in the forest. "I was under your stepmother's spell," he said, "but now she is gone forever."

Hansel and Gretel showed the woodcutter all the treasure. "We shall never be poor again," their father said, and they never were. As for the witch, it is said that you can still hear her cursing at the children from inside her old oven, deep in the thick, dark woods.

Rapunzel

Long ago, there lived a man and woman who were soon to have a baby. Each day, the woman gazed longingly at the garden next door, which was full of all sorts of flowers and plants that were good to eat. One plant, called rapunzel, made the woman's mouth water. "Please, husband," she said, "do fetch me some rapunzel. I have such a yearning for it. The plant is so very delicious and has such pretty blue flowers."

The woman's husband did not want to get the plant for his wife because the garden was owned by an old witch and he was afraid of her. "You must forget this nonsense," he said to his wife, but she asked him so many times, at last the man agreed.

One evening, the man climbed over the wall into the witch's garden. He had just grabbed a handful of the tender rapunzel when a furious voice said, "You dare to steal from me, thief!" It was the witch and she was angry.

The man explained all about his wife and their baby. "I'll strike a bargain with you," said the witch. "You may take the rapunzel, but in return you must give me your child when it is born." The man was so terrified, he agreed to the demands of the witch. Sure enough, when the child was born, the witch took her and named her Rapunzel.

Rapunzel

Rapunzel grew to be a beautiful young girl, who had long flowing hair, as golden as the sun.

The witch was jealous of Rapunzel's beauty, so she shut her in a tower on the edge of a great forest.

The tower had neither stairs nor a door, but only a little window at the top. Should the witch want to visit the girl she simply cried out, "Rapunzel, Rapunzel, let down your hair!"

As soon as Rapunzel heard the call, she unwound her thick, golden tresses and let them fall down as a rope for the witch to climb.

❧ *Rapunzel* ❧

Years passed and Rapunzel grew lonely in her solitude. Each day, she would sing a sweet, sad song to pass the time. The song was so lovely, the birds themselves could not have sung any more sweetly.

One day, a prince rode by and heard the beautiful singing, but could see no way to get into the tower. Then, he saw how the witch called to the girl and when she had gone, he did the same. "Rapunzel, Rapunzel, let down your hair!" he cried. Immediately, the golden hair tumbled down and the prince quickly climbed up to the window.

What a shock Rapunzel got when the prince appeared, but he spoke so softly to her and was so kind that she found herself falling in love with him.

Rapunzel

After that, the prince came to see Rapunzel every day. It was a great secret until, one day, the witch came to climb up Rapunzel's hair. The witch was so plump and clumsy that Rapunzel carelessly said, without thinking, "Oh, you are so much heavier than my prince. It is far harder to pull you up than he."

The witch's eyes narrowed angrily. "I thought I had cut you off from the world," she said, "but you have deceived me." With that, the wicked witch seized a sharp pair of scissors, grabbed Rapunzel's beautiful hair and with a swift *snip-snip*, chopped it clean off.

The witch used her powers to banish Rapunzel to the darkest depths of a great forest, in a faraway land. There, poor Rapunzel was even more lonely than before.

Meanwhile, the prince came to the bottom of the tower and called out, just as he had done each day before, "Rapunzel, Rapunzel, let down your hair."

The clever witch took the long braids of Rapunzel's hair and flung them out of the window.

When the prince climbed up, it was not the beautiful face of Rapunzel he saw, but the black-eyed, furious face of the ugly, old witch. With a cackle, she pushed the prince out of the window and he landed in a tangled thicket of thorns.

"You will never again see your true love," said the witch and she laughed at the prince as he lay bruised and bleeding on the ground.

Rapunzel

"Where is my Rapunzel?" cried the prince, but there was no reply. He stumbled into the silent woods and called and called, but still no one answered. On and on went the prince, wandering from place to place, searching for the girl he had fallen in love with.

Many months passed and the prince found himself in the middle of a great forest. He had searched and searched, but it seemed that Rapunzel was lost to him. In the forest, no bird sang or animal moved, there was only a hushed and empty silence. The prince sat down, put his head in his hands, and wept. Then, suddenly, he heard the faint sound of someone singing.

Rapunzel

The prince rushed through the dark trees, towards the sound of the beautiful voice that was so familiar to him. Bursting into a sunlit glade, he saw Rapunzel, sitting by a brook singing her sweet, sad song. The prince was overjoyed and Rapunzel was, too. "Can it really be true that we have found one another again?" she said.

"Yes, it is true," said the prince. "I shall take you far away from this place, where the witch cannot find you and you will always be safe."

The prince took Rapunzel to his kingdom and made her his wife. They lived happily together for the rest of their lives and were both very glad that they never set eyes on the wicked witch again.

The Elves and the Shoemaker

A cold wind whistled around the little shop where the poor shoemaker and his wife lived. The shoemaker sat at his bare workbench and gave a heavy sigh. "I only had enough money to buy leather for one pair of shoes," he said to his wife. "If I do not make and sell the shoes tomorrow, we shall starve, for there is no money left."

The shoemaker's wife lit the last candle they had. "Let us go to sleep," she said, "and we shall see what tomorrow brings." With that, the shoemaker and his wife went wearily to bed.

The night hours passed slowly and just before dawn, the shoemaker rose. He trudged down the creaking stairs to his little workshop and opened the door. To his amazement, there on the workbench was a beautiful pair of shoes. They had been cut and sewn so well, the shoemaker was sure he had never seen such fine workmanship. "What wonderful work!" cried the shoemaker, dancing about and laughing. "I am sure to sell these wonderful shoes today and we shall eat a good supper tonight. I wonder who could have done such a kind thing for us."

The Elves and the Shoemaker

The new shoes sold almost as soon as they went in the little shop window. The shoemaker made enough money to buy fine pink and blue leather and that night he and his wife had lovely food to eat for their supper. "We are very fortunate indeed," said the shoemaker. When it was time to go to bed, he left the piles of leather on his workbench and went upstairs.

The next morning, to their great surprise, the shoemaker and his wife found two pairs of beautiful shoes in the workshop. Once again, they put the shoes on display in the shop window. Soon, a rich lady and gentlemen came in to buy them. "What wonderful shoes," they said. "We have never seen the like of such workmanship and shall tell all our friends."

The shoemaker soon had enough money to buy the finest leather in the land. Each night, he would leave the leather in the little workshop and each morning there would be even more perfectly-made shoes than the night before. Soon, word of the talented shoemaker spread and people came from far and wide to buy his shoes.

Before long, the shoemaker and his wife made more money than they had ever dreamed of. "We will never be hungry again," said the shoemaker. He laughed and hugged his wife. "I can't remember when I felt so happy," he said. There was one thing, however, that both the shoemaker and his wife wanted to know more than anything. Who was it that had brought them such good fortune?

The Elves and the Shoemaker

That night, the shoemaker and his wife decided to find out who their nightly visitors were. As darkness fell, they hid behind a curtain and waited. The clock struck twelve and the shop bell tinkled softly as the door creaked open. There was a tiny pattering sound and suddenly, two small elves leapt up onto the workbench. They were dressed all in rags, but sang a cheery song as they set about threading needles and cutting out the leather. "Stitch and sew, stitch and sew. We will work and none shall know," they sang.

The elves snipped and sewed with such nimble fingers that it seemed to the shoemaker and his wife as if the finished shoes suddenly appeared before their eyes.

The Elves and the Shoemaker

"What a marvel it was to see the little fingers of those elves working so quickly," said the shoemaker, the next morning. "They have worked so hard, night after night, but asked nothing in return. I wish I could do something to repay them for their kindness."

The shoemaker's wife smiled. "There is something we can do," she said. "The elves looked so poor and ragged, a bit like we were before they came. Why don't we make them some new clothes?"

That very day, the shoemaker went out and bought expensive cloth, with fine gold thread to sew it and gleaming buttons, too. In the little workshop, the shoemaker and his wife stitched and sewed. Then, when night fell, they hid behind the curtain.

The Elves and the Shoemaker

The clock struck twelve and, just as before, the tinkle of the bell came as the shop door opened. The elves ran swiftly across the floor and jumped up on the workbench. This time, however, there were no piles of leather for them to work on through the night. Instead, folded in neat piles, were two lovely new suits and hats, finely sewn with delicate, gold thread. By the side of each pile was a tiny pair of the softest leather boots.

The elves were overjoyed. They put on their smart new clothes and smiled at one another. Then, the happy pair danced around, singing. "No more stitch and no more sew. We have new clothes, so it's time to go!"

Quick as a flash, the elves jumped off the workbench, scurried along the floor, and darted out of the shop, leaving the little shop bell tinkling behind them. The shoemaker and his wife did not mind that the elves had gone. "We have more than enough money now," said the shoemaker. In fact, the shoemaker had missed making shoes so much, he couldn't wait to get back to it.

The shoemaker and his wife lived happily ever after in their little shop. They never saw the elves again, but they were always grateful to them and knew that, out there somewhere, they would be dancing around in their new suits as happy as any little elves had ever been.

The Elves and the Shoemaker

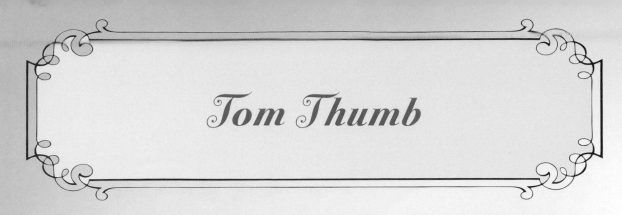

Tom Thumb

Once, in a faraway place, there was a man and woman who lived a poor and lonely life. "I wish we had children," said the man, "for our home is so lifeless without them." "I want a child more than anything in this world," replied his wife. "No matter how small it might be, I should love it with all my heart."

Such was the longing of the couple that some months later, they had a baby boy. He was perfect in every way, except that he was as tiny as a mouse and no matter how much he ate, the boy never grew bigger than a thumb. "We shall call you Tom Thumb," said the man and his wife.

One morning, the man got ready to go into the forest and chop wood. "Let me come, too, Father!" cried Tom. "I shall sit in the horse's ear and say, 'Giddy-up, giddy-up!'"
So, the man settled Tom into the horse's ear and he set off with a soft clip-clop down the forest path.

Now, it so happened that two traveling men heard the tiny voice saying, "Giddy-up, giddy-up," and when the cart stopped, they were astonished to see the tiny boy being lifted down from the horse's ear. "We could make our fortune showing him to people in the city," they said and offered the man a bag of gold in exchange for Tom Thumb.

Tom Thumb

Tom's father said that his son was more precious to him than all the gold in the world. However, Tom whispered into his father's ear, "Let me go, Papa. I promise I shall return soon." So, Tom hopped onto the brim of the hat of one of the traveling men, so that he could see all around him and they set off.

They had not gone far when Tom said, "Please let me down, for I need to rest a while." The man put Tom carefully onto the ground, but no sooner had he done so, than Tom dove down a mouse hole.

No matter how hard they tried, the two men could not find Tom Thumb. As dusk came, they gave up and went on their way, moaning about their wasted bag of gold.

Tom Thumb

Tom wriggled out of the mouse hole, but it was already getting dark. Owls hooted and foxes yapped. "It is not safe for me to be out here alone," Tom said to himself and he curled up inside an empty snail shell. He was just settling down for a nice sleep, when he overheard two robbers whispering about how they might steal gold and silver from a rich merchant's house nearby.

"I can help you," said Tom Thumb, jumping out from his snail shell, and he laughed at the surprised faces of the two robbers.

"How could someone as small as you do that?" asked the robbers.

"Why, I will crawl through a gap under the door and open a window for you," said Tom.

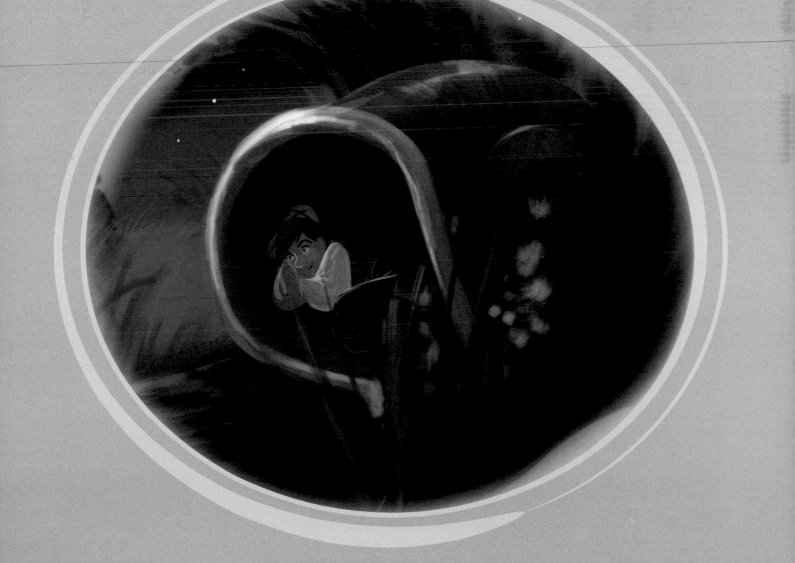

Tom and the robbers went to the merchant's house. Just as he had promised, Tom crept under the door into the silent kitchen and opened the window. Once inside, Tom called as loudly as he could to the robbers, "Are you going to take all the silver and the gold, too?"

"Shhh, speak softly or you shall wake everyone in the house," said the robbers.

Tom did not speak softly, however. Instead, he roared at the top of his voice.

"There is plenty in here to fill a robber's sack. You shall not be disappointed!"

Tom shouted so loudly, he woke the sleeping merchant who ran downstairs, shouting, "Thieves, thieves!" The two robbers got such a fright, they fled into the night as if a wolf was chasing them.

As for Tom Thumb, the merchant was amazed to see such a tiny young man. He listened as Tom told him all about his poor parents and the story of his adventures. Then Tom told the merchant how he had come to warn him of the two robbers.

The merchant was very grateful to Tom. He rewarded him handsomely with a big bag of gold and sent him back home in a gilded carriage.

Tom's parents were overjoyed to see him. They were never poor again and lived a long and happy life. As for Tom, he had more adventures than could ever be told and he was always proud to be famous for being the boy who was no bigger than a thumb.

Snow White

Long ago, as snowflakes drifted from a winter sky, a queen made a wish to have a child with skin as white as snow, lips as red as blood, and hair as black as night. "I shall call her Snow White," said the queen. Sure enough, the queen had a baby girl, but soon after the child was born, the queen died.

The king loved his little daughter, but soon he grew lonely and decided to marry again. His new wife was a beautiful, but cruel woman who had a magic mirror. Each day, the queen looked in the mirror and asked, "Mirror, mirror, on the wall. Who is the fairest of them all?"
"You are the fairest of them all," replied the mirror.
The vain queen was happy, for she knew that the mirror always told the truth.

Years passed and Snow White grew into a beautiful young girl. With each passing day, the queen grew more and more envious of her stepdaughter and hatred grew in her heart. One day, she stood in front of her magic mirror and asked, "Mirror, mirror on the wall, who is the fairest of them all?" The queen waited and then the mirror spoke. "Snow White is the fairest of them all," it said.

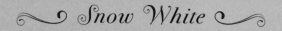

The angry queen summoned her huntsman. "Take Snow White into the woods and kill her!" she screamed. "Do not come back here until she is dead."

The huntsman took Snow White deep into the dark woods, but he was a kind man and he took pity on the girl. "Run, Snow White," he said. "Run and don't look back."
The huntsman returned to the wicked queen, but lied to her when he said he had killed Snow White.

Snow White ran deeper into the forest. Thorns and brambles scratched her legs, but still she ran on. "What shall become of me?" she sobbed, as the wind moaned in the trees and the setting sun cast shadows along the path.

At last, Snow White came upon a cottage in a clearing. Inside, she found a little table set with seven plates and seven knives and forks. By the fireside were seven little beds. Exhausted from running, Snow White lay down on one and slept.

As night fell, Snow White was awoken by the sound of whistling in the forest. Suddenly, the cottage door flew open and in marched seven dwarves. "Forgive me," said Snow White, crying. "I had nowhere else to go." The dwarves listened quietly as Snow White told them her story. "Stay with us," they said. "You will be safe here, but remember never to answer the door to strangers." So, Snow White stayed with the seven dwarves and for a time at least, she was happy.

❦ Snow White ❧

At the palace, the evil queen laughed cruelly and admired her own cold beauty. She was sure that Snow White was dead. "No one will ever be as beautiful as me," she said and turning to her mirror she asked, "Mirror, mirror, on the wall, who is the fairest of them all?"

"Snow White is the fairest of them all," replied the mirror and it showed snow white in the forest where she lived with the seven dwarves. The queen trembled with rage.

"I will put an end to you, Snow White," she hissed and with that, transformed herself into an old woman. Then, the wicked queen filled a basket with apples and got a bottle of poison.

The queen set off into the forest with the basket full of apples. One was bigger and more juicy than the rest, but half of it was poisoned.

Tap-tap, went the queen on the door of the cottage. Snow White forgot the dwarves' warning and she opened the door. "A juicy, ripe apple for you, my dear?" said the old woman.

Snow White hesitated, then she reached out and grasping the shiny red apple, she took a bite.

In an instant, Snow White fell to the floor, her face as pale as death. The wicked queen celebrated wickedly and then disappeared into the woods.

Snow White

That evening, the happy dwarves came home to find Snow White lying as if dead. Their happiness turned to sorrow as they cried for their lost friend. "We will lay her in the forest," they said, sadly, "where the birds and the animals can see her." For Snow White looked just as if she was sleeping, with her lips as red as blood, skin as white as snow, and hair as black as night.

So the dwarves carried Snow White into the forest. They lay her in a glass coffin, for she was too beautiful to put in the cold, dark earth. Each day the dwarves went to visit Snow White and watched over their dear friend.

One day, when the new leaves of spring had emerged, a prince came riding through the forest. He came to the place where Snow White lay and was astonished. "She is the most beautiful girl I have ever seen," he said. Thinking Snow White was asleep, the prince bent down and gave her a single kiss on her cheek. As if by magic, Snow White opened her eyes.

"She lives!" cried the dwarves and they were overjoyed.

The prince and Snow White fell in love and were soon married. As for the wicked queen, it is said that on hearing that Snow White was still alive, she smashed her magic mirror into a thousand pieces and disappeared, never to be seen again.

The Golden Goose

Once there was a man who had three sons. One day, the eldest son set off into the forest to chop wood. "Take this cake and juice," said his mother, "so you will not go hungry or thirsty while you are walking."

The eldest son set off into the forest. He had not gone far when he met an old man. "May I have some of your cake and juice?" he asked. "I am hungry and thirsty."
"No," said the eldest son, "for I shall have none for myself!" and he began to chop wood. Before long, however, the ax blade slipped and struck him on the arm, so he had to return home.

The second son went into the forest next and took some cake and juice for himself. He too met the little old man, but refused to share either his food or drink. Then, as he was chopping wood, the blade slipped and struck his leg, so he had to return home.

"I shall get the wood," said the youngest son, but his brothers just laughed at him. "You are far too stupid to succeed!" they cried together.

There were only rough biscuits and water left for the youngest son, but he took them and set off. Sure enough, he came across the old man who asked him if he would share what he had.
"Of course I will," said the youngest son and he offered all he had to the old man.
"You have a good heart," said the man, "and for that, I will give you good luck. Cut down that old tree over there and see what you find."

So, the youngest son cut down the tree and inside, was a goose that had feathers of pure gold.

The Golden Goose

The youngest son picked up the golden goose and walked on through the woods. After quite some time, he came across an inn and thought he might stay there for the night.

Now, the innkeeper had three daughters who were very curious. "If only we could each have a feather from that golden goose!" they cried.

As soon as the youngest son had gone to bed, the eldest sister crept downstairs and grabbed the golden goose by the wing. However, when she tried to pull a feather out, her fingers stuck fast.

The second sister came soon afterwards, but no sooner had she touched her sister, than she was stuck too. The same thing happened with the third sister, until all three were stuck like glue.

The Golden Goose

The next morning, the youngest son did not trouble himself when he found the three sisters stuck to his golden goose, but simply tucked the goose under his arm and went on his way.

In a grassy meadow, a farmer saw the boy with the golden goose and three girls trailing behind. As they passed him, he took the hand of the youngest sister and had scarcely touched her, when he too became stuck. What a strange procession they made! One behind the other they went and the farmer called to his wife, "Set me free!" Once again, no sooner had the farmer's wife touched her husband, than she too joined the line.

The Golden Goose

On and on went the boy with the golden goose and his five companions, over the hill and into the town. "Help!" they cried, so loudly that the butcher came to look and the baker, too! Very soon, both were stuck like the sisters and the farmer and his wife before them, all trotting after the boy with the golden goose.

Before long, they came to a kingdom where a princess lived who was so serious that no one could ever make her happy. "Whoever can make her laugh can marry her!" declared the king.

The youngest son liked the look of the princess, so he went with his goose and the strange band of people and paraded before her. The princess had never seen anything as funny as the seven people, all stuck together in a line. She thought it was so amusing, she laughed as though she would never stop.

The princess made such a loud noise that the golden goose flapped her wings and immediately, everyone who was stuck became unstuck. They all fell into a heap on the floor, which only made the princess laugh even more. Luckily, the princess fell in love with the youngest son and everyone was sure that they would live happily ever after, with their lucky golden goose.

The Frog Prince

Once, a princess sat by a pond playing with a shining, golden ball. The princess threw the ball in the air and held out her hand to catch it, but it landed with a splash in the water and sank to the bottom. The princess was very upset because the ball was her most precious thing. She cried and cried and would not be comforted.

"Why do you cry, Princess?" said a voice. "Even a rock would feel pity for you."
The princess looked all around and then she saw a big, ugly frog sticking its head out of the water.
"I have lost my golden ball," she said, "and that is why I am weeping."

"If I get your ball," said the frog, "what will you promise me in return?"
"You may have my dresses and jewels and even my crown," replied the princess.
The frog did not want jewels or clothes. "I wish only to be your companion," he said.
"I wish to sit at your table, eat off your golden plate, drink from your cup, and sleep in your royal bed."
"I promise that you shall have your wishes," said the princess.

With that, the frog dove down, down to the bottom of the pond. No sooner had he brought the golden ball up, however, than the princess grabbed it and ran away. She had no intention of fulfilling a promise made to a silly, slimy frog.

The Frog Prince

The next day, the princess was eating her supper at the royal table when there was a small knock at the door. "Princess, let me in," said a croaky voice.

The princess opened the door and saw the little frog. "Ugh, it's you!" she cried. "Go away!"

"My child, what is the matter?" asked the king.

The princess explained about the lost, golden ball and her promise to the frog.

The king looked at his daughter and frowned. "You have made a promise," he said, "and you must keep it." So, the unhappy princess let the frog into the royal banquet hall, where he ate from her plate and drank from her cup.

When he had finished, the frog gave a big yawn. "I wish you to carry me to your royal bedchamber and we shall go to sleep," he said to the princess.

The princess began to cry. She did not want to touch this cold, slimy creature, let alone think of him sleeping in her lovely, clean bed!

"You will do as the frog asks," demanded the king. "For no daughter of mine shall break a promise." The princess reluctantly took the frog upstairs to her bed. He slept on the soft pillow next to her until the light of dawn streamed in through the bedroom window.

As the princess woke, the frog began to croak. "Kiss me, princess," he said. "Kiss me and I shall leave you alone forever."

The princess could not wait to get rid of the ugly frog, so she reached out and placed a reluctant kiss on his cold, slippery skin. "Yuck!" she said, wiping her mouth. "Now go away and leave me alone, you disgusting frog." With that, the princess flung the pillow on which the frog sat across the room and it landed with a soft thud.

The Frog Prince

There was silence and the princess wondered if she had hurt the frog. "Are you alright?" she asked. "Yes, thank you," came the reply, but it was not the croaky voice of the frog. There, in place of the frog was a handsome, young man. "I am a prince," he said, "and an evil witch cursed me and turned me into a frog. Only the kiss of a princess would set me free."

The princess was very happy that there was no longer a horrid, ugly frog in her bedroom. She fell in love with the prince and of course, they did live happily ever after.

Sleeping Beauty

Long ago, in the hall of a grand palace, a king and queen held a great feast to celebrate the birth of their baby daughter. Among the finely dressed guests were three wise fairies who brought magical gifts for the little princess. One fairy gave her beauty and another gave her kindness. The third fairy was just about to give her gift when there was a terrible screeching noise. Suddenly, an angry fairy burst into the feast. The king had forgotten to invite her and she was very angry. "You dare to ignore me?" cried the fairy. "Well, I have my own gift to give. On her fifteenth birthday, your precious daughter will prick her finger on a spindle and fall down dead." The fairy gave a wicked laugh and disappeared from the silent hall.

The guests stared at one another in amazement and the queen burst into tears. Just then, the third fairy stepped forward. "I cannot undo this dark magic," she said, "but my wish is that the princess shall not die, but instead fall into a deep sleep for one hundred years."

The king was comforted by the third fairy's gift, but he so feared that harm might come to his daughter, he commanded that every spindle in the kingdom be destroyed.

Many years passed and the wishes of the first two fairies came true. The princess grew to be a beautiful and kind young woman. On the morning of her fifteenth birthday, everyone was busy preparing a party for the princess, so she wandered off to explore the oldest parts of the palace.

Empty corridors and hallways echoed with the footsteps of the princess and a chill crept over her. The princess was about to turn back when she noticed a narrow staircase winding upwards. "I wonder where it goes?" thought the curious princess as she tiptoed up the steps. At the top was a little door with a key in the lock.

Sleeping Beauty

The princess turned the key and the door creaked open. There, in a small room, was a bed, beside which, an old woman sat at a spindle, busily spinning flax. The princess greeted the old woman and smiled. "What are you doing?" she asked, for the princess had never seen a spindle before. "I am spinning," said the old woman. "Come and try, my dear," she said.

The princess reached out to hold the spindle. No sooner had she touched it, than she pricked her finger and the magic spell of the angry fairy came true. In that very moment, the princess fell down upon the bed and lay in a deep sleep.

Sleeping Beauty

The sleeping spell fell upon the entire palace, enchanted by the angry fairy. Horses slept in their stables and the cook snored in the kitchen. In the great hall, the fire sputtered out and the king and the queen fell asleep on their thrones. A deathly hush fell everywhere and all was silent. As time went on, brambles grew along the pathways and crept up the cold stone walls. Soon, the splendid palace became covered in a tangle of thorns.

Years passed and many had heard the story of the sleeping princess. Some had even tried to free her, but the web of thorns was like a million tightly-clasped hands that grasped at those who tried to free them.

Then, on the exact day that one hundred years had passed, a prince came to the enchanted palace. He had heard of the beautiful princess and of those before him who had failed to find her. "I am not afraid," he said, as he drew his glinting sword and began to cut away at the thick wall of thorns. As if by magic, the thorns began to part and beautiful flowers bloomed. The prince passed safely through the barbed curtain, into the palace courtyard. Nothing stirred and everywhere was still under the quiet spell of sleep.

Sleeping Beauty

Inside the palace, the prince looked in every corridor and chamber. The king and queen still slept on their thrones and the cook slumbered in the kitchen. The mice were curled in their holes and the servants slumped in the hallways.

At last, the prince came to the room where the princess slept. There she lay, so beautiful the prince could hardly take his eyes off her. "So you are Sleeping Beauty," he said and stooped down to give her a single kiss. As he did, the princess opened her eyes and looked at him so sweetly that he instantly fell in love with her.

Sleeping Beauty

At that very moment, the spell was lifted from the palace and everyone woke up. Horses neighed in the stable and the court dogs wagged their tails. In the kitchen, the cook stirred the broth. In the great hall, the king and queen yawned as the flames sprang up once again in the grate.

The sleeping palace came back to life. There was great joy and happiness at the news that the prince and princess were to be married. A celebration, the like of which the palace had never seen, was held and everyone lived happily until the end of their days.

Rumpelstiltskin

Long ago, there lived a poor miller who wanted to impress the king so much, he told him that his daughter could spin straw into gold. "This idea pleases me," said the king, for even though he was rich, he was a very greedy man.

The king had the miller's daughter brought to the palace, where he took her to a room full of straw. He gave the girl a spinning wheel. "Work hard," said the king, "and turn this straw to gold by sunrise tomorrow. If you do not, then I shall put you in my dungeon." With that, the king locked the door and left the girl alone.

"What am I to do?" said the miller's daughter in dismay. "I cannot spin straw into gold." The girl thought of the task before her and began to weep. Just then, a strange little man appeared from thin air. "Good evening, my dear," he said with a strange smile. "Why are you crying?"

The girl explained all about the king's request and the little man thought for a moment. "I can spin straw into gold," he said, "but what will you give me if I do?" "I will give you my necklace," replied the girl. The little man took the necklace and sat down at the spindle. *Click, whirr, whirr,* it went, hour after hour, until, by morning, the room was full of the finest gold thread.

Rumpelstiltskin

At sunrise, the king was astonished to see the perfectly-spun gold. At once, his heart was filled with greed and he immediately took the miller's daughter to a bigger room that was also full of straw. "Spin this straw to gold by sunrise," he commanded, "if you value your life." The girl was twice as frightened and fearing that the king would keep his promise, she began to cry. Suddenly, just as on the previous night, the little man appeared from nowhere. Once again, he asked the girl what she would give him if he turned the straw into gold for her.

"I will give you my ring," said the girl. So, the little man took the ring, began to turn the wheel and, by morning, had spun the straw into glistening gold.

⌁ ✣ *Rumpelstiltskin* ✣ ⌁

The king was so overjoyed when he saw the spun gold, he wanted even more and took the girl to a much larger room with more straw in it. "If you can spin this straw to gold, I shall make you my wife," he said.

For a third time, the strange little man appeared to help the miller's daughter, but this time, she had nothing left to give to him. "Once you become queen," said the man, "You must promise to give me your firstborn child." The miller's daughter did not really believe that the greedy king would marry her, so she agreed to the little man's request. Just as before, he sat at the spindle all night and by morning, the straw was spun into gold.

The princesses danced with the princes for hours while the soldier watched from under his cloak. The room was full of laughter and smiles as the girls whirled and twirled around and around. It looked like so much fun that the soldier would have liked to have joined in. He was especially fond of the youngest princess, who kept looking over her shoulder, certain that something felt different that night.

When the time finally came for them to go home, the princesses waved goodbye to the princes. They journeyed back over the lake, through the trees of diamonds, gold, and silver and back to their beds where they snuggled up, safe and warm.

The next morning, the soldier stood before the king and told him all that he had seen. He gave the king the twigs, flowers, and leaves he had taken from the enchanted forests and pointed to the girls' tattered shoes. The king was so happy to finally have an answer to his daughters' secret, he told the soldier that as a reward, he could pick one of the princesses to wed. The soldier chose the youngest princess to marry and when he asked her if she would do him the honor of becoming his wife, she replied, "Yes," smiling happily. "A man clever enough to discover our secret will make a worthy husband."

The soldier and the princess were married soon after, and everyone who was invited to the wedding danced through the night, until their shoes were all worn out!

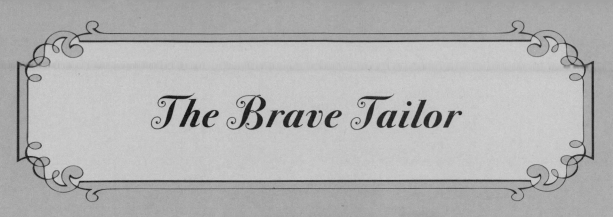

The Brave Tailor

One morning, a little tailor was trying to enjoy his breakfast when a number of flies came buzzing around his pot of jam. The tailor was so annoyed that he swatted the flies and seven of them fell onto his table.

The tailor thought he was so clever to have swatted so many flies all at once that he made himself a belt into which he stitched the words, 'Seven in one blow.'
"I shall go out into the world," said the tailor, "for I am far too brave for this tiny shop."

So, the tailor put a fresh cheese in his pocket and took his little pet bird and placed her in there, too. He went out of the town and had just reached the top of a hill when he saw a scary-looking giant sitting on a rock. "Hello," said the tailor, suddenly feeling nervous.

"What do you want?" boomed the giant, angrily. Then, he peered at the tailor and his strange belt. Reading the words on the belt, the giant thought the tailor had killed seven men in one blow. "Surely this cannot be true," the giant said. Then, he took a rock in his fist and crushed it until it cracked into pieces. "Beat that if you can," he boasted.

The tailor put his hand into his pocket. He took out the cheese and, pretending it was a stone, he squeezed it until the liquid ran out of it. "See how I squeeze water from this stone!" he cried.

The giant didn't like the thought of a little tailor being so much stronger than him and he decided to do something about it. The giant invited the tailor to come to the cave where he lived. After supper, the giant said to the little tailor, "You may sleep in that bed over there." The tailor went over to the bed, but it was so big that he decided to sleep in a dark corner of the cave instead.

In the dead of night, thinking that the tailor was fast asleep in the bed, the giant crept up and grabbed the sheets. With one enormous swing, he hurled the sheets out of the cave and into the darkness. "Ha! ha!" he chuckled, "that is the end of you, little tailor," and with that, the giant went back to sleep.

The Brave Tailor

The next day, at dawn, the giant was so busy looking for his breakfast in the forest, that he had quite forgotten about the tailor. He was snuffling around, looking for truffles when suddenly, the tailor stepped out from behind a tree. "Good morning, Giant," he said. "Did you have a pleasant night?"

The giant was so shocked at the sight of the little tailor that he began to feel afraid. "I am no match for you!" he cried and he ran away, making the ground shake, never to return again. As for the little tailor, he carried on with his journey and had many adventures along the way, just as you would expect of a man who had killed seven in one blow.

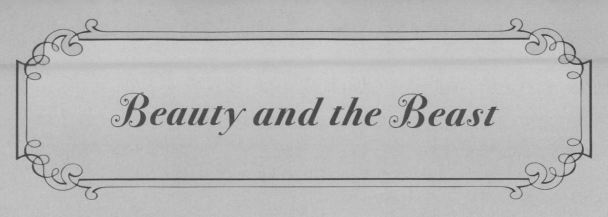

Beauty and the Beast

In a tiny cottage in the country, there once lived a merchant who had very little money. The merchant's ships had been sunk in a great storm and all but one was lost.

"I must go to the city and tend to my business," the merchant said to his three daughters. "Is there anything that you would like me to bring back for you?"

"Bring us dresses and jewels, Father!" cried two of the daughters, for they were spoiled and selfish and thought nothing of their father's troubles. The third daughter, Beauty, was kind and she loved her father dearly. She alone had seen the worried look on her father's face, so she said, "All I ask for is a simple rose, Father."

The merchant kissed his daughters and set off for the city. When he got there, he found that his one remaining ship had been sold to pay off the money he owed. Weary and exhausted, the merchant began the long journey home. He walked for hours and had just entered some dark woods, when a wild storm began to blow. Jagged lightning flashed and grumbling thunder rumbled and the merchant soon found that he was lost. Then, a shock of dazzling lightning lit up the sky and he saw a beautiful palace.

The merchant was so very tired and wet that he sought shelter in the palace. As the great door creaked open, he entered a hall in which a warm fire blazed.

Near the fireside was a table set with one gold plate, beside which was a single gold goblet, full of wine. All around the table were dishes of delicious food and the merchant was so hungry, he could not help but sit down and eat. Then, when he had finished, he went upstairs to find a room where a freshly-made bed was waiting. "It is as if I was expected," said the merchant and he fell into a deep, dreamless sleep.

Beauty and the Beast

The next morning, as the merchant was leaving the palace, he noticed a pretty rose garden. Suddenly, he remembered Beauty's simple request for a rose, so he reached out and plucked a perfect red bloom. No sooner had he done so, than there was a terrible roar and a hideous beast appeared, flashing glinting, white teeth. "You dare to steal my roses, after I have shown you such kindness," growled the beast. "For this, you must die."

The terrified merchant told the beast the story of how he had left his daughters to come to the city. "I will give you fine dresses and jewels for your daughters," said the beast, "but in exchange, you must return to my palace and live here."

The merchant fled back to his home. He told his daughters all about his bargain with the beast. The two spoiled ones were so overjoyed with the dresses and jewels, they cared nothing for what became of their father. Beauty, however, cared very much. Early the next morning, she crept out of the cottage and traveled to the palace of the beast.

The beast greeted Beauty, graciously. He gave her lavish clothing and food and each evening, they sat by the fire together and talked, long into the night. Beauty was so kind and gentle that the beast fell in love with her and said he would give her anything that her heart desired.

Months passed and the beast gave Beauty many beautiful things, but there was one thing she desired above all else. "I want to go home and see my family," she said.

The beast felt very sad. "I will agree to this," he said, "but you must promise to return within one week." The beast gave Beauty a magic mirror so that she could see his palace and a ring that would bring her back there in an instant.

"Do not be afraid," said Beauty to the beast, "for I promise that I shall return," and with that, she set off on the long journey home.

Beauty's father was overjoyed to see his lovely daughter, but her sisters were very jealous. They envied Beauty's life with the beast and wanted to spoil it. When a week had passed, they pretended to cry and said, "Oh, please, Beauty, do not leave us yet," but secretly, they hoped that on her return to the palace, the beast would be very angry and kill their sister.

Beauty agreed to stay longer with her family, but as time passed, she thought more and more of the beast and his kindness to her. Then, one night when the full moon shone, she thought she heard a howl of pain. Beauty looked in the magic mirror and saw the beast lying motionless under the rose bush her father had plucked the rose from.

Beauty and the Beast

Beauty looked at the magic ring. "Take me back to the beast!" she cried.

In an instant, Beauty was back at the palace. She ran to the rose garden and found the beast lying on the ground. Beauty held him in her arms. "Forgive me for breaking my promise," she sobbed. "I love you and I will never leave you again."

Suddenly, the beast began to change. A golden light shimmered around him and he transformed into a handsome young man. He smiled at Beauty. "I am a prince who was enchanted by a wicked witch. Your love has set me free and we will never be parted again."

Beauty married her prince and they had a wonderful wedding. Just as the prince had promised, they lived happily ever after and were never parted again.

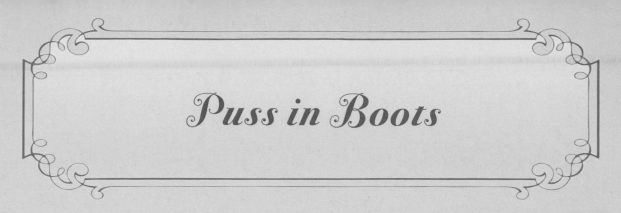

Puss in Boots

Long ago, there lived a miller who wanted to give something to each of his three beloved sons. "To my eldest son, I give my mill. To my second son, I give my two mules," said the miller. Then, he came to his youngest son, "All I have left for you is my cat," he said, sadly.

The youngest son was very disappointed. How could he make his way in the world with only a cat? "I shall surely starve," he said, but then, to his complete amazement, the cat began to speak. "Do not fear, Master," said the cat. "If you will only give me a pair of boots, I promise that I shall make you into a prince."

The son was astonished, but nonetheless, he spent the few gold coins he had left on a gleaming pair of new leather boots and gave them to the cat.

The cat immediately went off to the woods and caught several rabbits to present to the king. The king was very impressed with the gift from the cat. "Who is your master?" the king asked.

The clever cat wanted to make the king think that the miller's son was someone very important. "Why, my master is the Marquis of Carabas," he replied.

For months afterwards, the cat brought the king plump little birds and fat, juicy rabbits. The king was very pleased with the gifts and most impressed by the cat and his mysterious master, the Marquis of Carabas.

Puss in Boots

One morning, the king told the cat that he wanted his daughter to marry the Marquis of Carabas and that he would travel to see the Marquis that very day.

The cunning cat ran home and persuaded his bewildered master to remove all of his clothes and stand in the river. The cat was hiding the clothes beneath a rock, when he heard the clip-clop of horses' hooves as they pulled the royal coach over the bridge above.

"Help! Help!" cried the cat, as loud as he could. "The Marquis of Carabas was bathing in the river and someone has stolen his clothes!"

The king had the young man brought from the river and dressed him in a splendid suit of clothes. Then, he seated the young man in the royal coach with his daughter, the princess. As soon as the miller's son and the princess saw one another, they fell in love.

Meanwhile, the clever cat hurried ahead of the coach. In the fields, the summer grass was being cut and gathered by farm workers. "The king is coming," said the cat, "and you must tell him that this land belongs to the Marquis of Carabas, otherwise he will put you in the palace dungeons."

The poor field hands were so frightened that they did exactly what was asked of them.

Further along the road, the cat came upon a castle where a fierce ogre lived. It was said that the ogre had magical powers and could change himself into any type of animal he wished.

Tap, tap, went the cat on the castle door. Thunderous steps shook the ground and the ugly ogre jerked the door open. "What do you want?" he bellowed.

"Is is true that you have the power to transform yourself into different animals?" asked the cat. "Yes," replied the ogre, flattered that someone was taking an interest in him. Suddenly, he transformed himself into a huge lion and chased the cat all over the castle.

"That's very impressive," said the cat, "but I bet you can't change yourself into something as small as a mouse."

The ogre grunted. "Of course I can," he said. With that, the ogre became a mouse, and the clever cat gobbled him up with one quick gulp.

~♥~ Puss in Boots ~♥~

Clip-clop, clip-clop, went the horses' hooves as the king's coach arrived at the ogre's castle. The king thought the castle belonged to the miller's son, for it was very fine indeed and he had no hesitation in offering his daughter's hand in marriage to the young man he thought of as the Marquis of Carabas.

The miller's son married a princess and became a prince. He was always grateful to his puss in boots and enjoyed a life of luxury. As for the cat, he got a new, even smarter pair of boots and as many mice as he could chase and it goes without saying that he lived happily ever after.

Aladdin

Under the eastern sky, where the stars shone like sparkling jewels, there once lay a hidden cave filled with vast hoards of treasure. Legend told of a magic lamp inside the cave that would bring the owner great fortune, but most were too scared to search for it, in case they got caught in one of the cave's many traps. An evil magician named Mustafa wanted the lamp for himself, but instead of risking his own life, he tricked a beggar boy, called Aladdin, to go in his place. "If you bring back the lamp for me," Mustafa said to the boy, "then the rest of the treasure is yours."

Mustafa stood at the entrance of the cave, his eyes gleaming with greed as he watched Aladdin find the tarnished, old lamp. Just as Aladdin was about to step out of the cave, Mustafa grabbed the lamp out of his hands and pushed a boulder in front of the entrance to trap the boy inside. At the last second, Mustafa's hand slipped and the lamp tumbled into the cave. "NOOO!" he cried in dismay.

Trapped in the darkness, Aladdin fumbled around, accidentally rubbing the lamp. The lamp glowed faintly and a genie suddenly appeared in a puff of blue smoke. "I am the genie of the lamp," he said. "I am here to grant your every wish." "Can you help me get out of this cave?" asked Aladdin. "Of course! I can do anything," replied the genie and with a sparkling flash, he freed them both.

∾ Aladdin ∾

Aladdin was devastated to find that he had lost everything to Mustafa. The princess was upset, too, realizing the mistake she had made by giving up the lamp. In order to fix things, she quickly came up with a clever plan.

That night, she pretended that she was happy to be Mustafa's wife. "Let's have a party to celebrate," she said, laying out a grand table of food and drinks. Mustafa was pleased that the princess preferred him to the beggar boy, Aladdin, and sat down to enjoy the fabulous feast. All the eating and merriment made Mustafa very tired and soon, he fell fast asleep. Then, the princess let Aladdin into the palace and they took back the magic lamp.

Together, they rubbed the lamp and summoned the genie to appear. "Genie," they said. "Please undo Mustafa's wish and return everything to the way it was."

"Your wish is my command," said the genie, happily. With a flick of his hand, he sent sparkles of magic whirling and twirling into the air. The palace went back to normal again, Aladdin was restored to his rightful place as future king and Mustafa was magically banished from the kingdom. Soon, everything was once again as it should be, and Aladdin and the princess lived happily together from that day on.

꩜ *Thumbelina* ꩜

The lily pad drifted along on the water. As the sun came up, the water glittered like gold. "How pretty it is," thought Thumbelina. She felt very glad that she had escaped from that ugly toad.

Just then, a yellow butterfly fluttered past. Thumbelina quickly tied some ribbon from her dress to its feet and the butterfly pulled the lily pad even faster downstream. Thumbelina was just beginning to enjoy the many things she saw on the river bank when suddenly, a huge beetle swooped down and grabbed her by the waist. It lifted her off the lily pad and flew off with her into the trees.

Little Thumbelina was very frightened and became even more so when she saw all the other beetles in the tree. "What is this you have brought to us?" they said, laughing. "It is rather ugly and looks like a tiny human. We have no use for such a strange-looking creature."

The beetle who had grabbed Thumbelina did not wish to upset his family. "I have no use for you either, little creature," he said, and grabbing Thumbelina once again, he flew out of the tree and set her down near a patch of daisies in the forest. Poor Thumbelina cried and cried, for she did not want to be thought of as ugly.

~ᑌ᠊ Thumbelina ᠊ᑌ~

All summer long, Thumbelina lived alone. She slept in a bed made of leaves under a big, broad green leaf. She scooped nectar from the flowers and drank dew from the morning grass. Too soon, however, winter came. The sharp frost chilled Thumbelina's bones and she shivered with cold. "I must leave this place," she said, "or I shall surely freeze to death."

So, Thumbelina set off. A little way beyond the forest, she came across a meadow in which a field mouse lived. His little house was snug and warm and the rich smell of delicious roasting nuts wafted in the air. Thumbelina was so hungry, she knocked on the door of the little house where the field mouse lived and asked if she could go in.

♥ *Thumbelina* ♥

The field mouse was very kind to Thumbelina. "If you clean for me and tell me stories, I will give you a home," he said. So, Thumbelina worked happily for the field mouse. She even made friends with an injured swallow who had nearly perished in the cold. She wrapped him up warmly and fed him until the spring came and he was able to fly free once more.

Thumbelina was very happy, until one day, a mole came to call. He was a bossy, grumpy creature who, at one glance, fell in love with Thumbelina and decided to marry her. He wanted her to live in his underground home, so that she would never see the sunshine again.

Thumbelina

Thumbelina was terribly upset. "What am I to do?" she said to the spring flowers and the trees. "Even the field mouse wants me to marry the mole. If only my swallow friend was here to help me."

Suddenly, there was a twittering from the trees. "Here I am," said the swallow. "Jump on my back, Thumbelina, and we will fly far away from here."
Thumbelina was overjoyed to see her friend. She quickly jumped on his back and they flew, up, up into the blue sky.

The bird flew far away with Thumbelina, over fields and trees, until they reached a lush forest where the most beautiful white flowers grew. The swallow set Thumbelina down on one of the flowers and said, "This will be your home now."

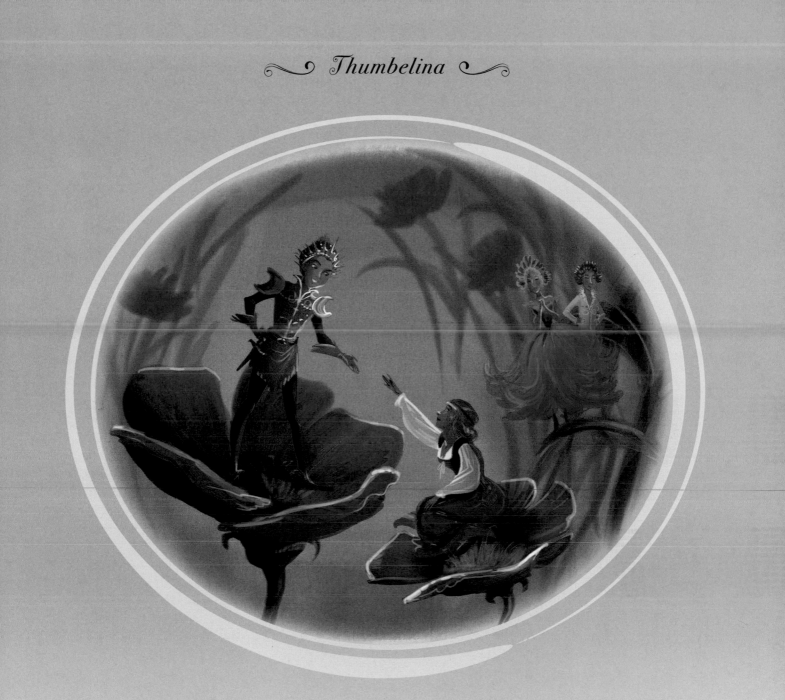

How astonished the tiny girl was when she saw the petals of a nearby flower open to reveal a tiny man, no bigger than herself! He had a gold crown on his head and he smiled at Thumbelina who was enchanted and thought him very beautiful.

"I am King of the Flowers," said the little man, smiling. He, in turn, was enchanted by Thumbelina. He took the gold crown from his head and placed it on hers. "Will you be my queen?" he asked.

"Yes," said Thumbelina, for she had fallen instantly in love with the king.

There was much rejoicing and high in the trees, the little swallow sang his happy song as Thumbelina became the beautiful queen of all the flowers.

Snow White and Rose Red

There once was a poor widow who lived in a little cottage with her daughters, Snow White and Rose Red. One winter's night, they were reading stories by the crackling fire when there was a knock at the door. "It must be a traveler, seeking shelter," said the widow, but when she opened the door, there stood a big brown bear.

The widow and her daughters screamed in fright, but then the bear began to speak. "Do not be afraid," he said, "for I shall not hurt you. I am half frozen and only want to warm myself a little."

The bear spoke so softly, the widow felt sorry for him and let him in. The bear warmed himself by the fire and began to tell Snow White and Rose Red wonderful tales of his many adventures. The girls liked him instantly and soon they were giggling and playing games together. "You must visit us each night," they said, "for it is a very cold winter." The bear agreed and each night after that, he came to the little cottage. Soon, the bear became good friends with Rose Red and her sister, Snow White.

Before long, the spring came. "I must leave you," said the bear, "for a wicked dwarf has stolen my treasure from me and I must get it back."
Snow White and Rose Red said goodbye to their friend and they felt sad at the thought that they might never see him again.

The Six Swans

The king was very sad, but he had no choice but to imprison his queen in the dungeons. "I must banish you from this kingdom forever," he said. If the queen spoke a single word to the king, it would mean that her brothers remained as swans forever. So, she simply stared at her husband dumbly as tears ran down her cheeks. "You shall be taken away first thing tomorrow morning," said the king and he left his wife alone, still sewing the last of the flax shirts.

The next day was the last day of the six years during which the girl was not allowed to speak. She had faithfully sewn the six shirts and as she was taken out of the palace, she held them tightly in her hands. "Goodbye," said the king, his heart heavy with sadness.

The queen was just about to be taken away by the royal guards when suddenly she heard a great beating of wings in the sky. Six beautiful swans swept towards her and as they landed near her, the young queen put a shirt on each one. As if by magic, they transformed into her handsome brothers.

The Six Swans

The spell was broken and at last the queen was able to speak. "I am innocent," she said to the king and she explained how his mother had stolen the children. The king was astonished, but overjoyed that his queen did not have to be banished.

"Forgive me for doubting you," he said.

Immediately, the king ordered the royal guards to search the palace. It was not long before the twin daughters and baby son were found unharmed and brought back to their parents.

Now that the queen's brothers had been transformed back into human form, they were very happy that they would never again have to live as swans or under a curse. As for the king's evil mother, she was banished to a faraway land and never heard from again.

Peace returned to the kingdom and at last, as in all good fairy tales, everyone lived happily ever after.